A Day with Yayah

Written in loving memory of Auntie "E.I." Ethel Isaac
for our childhood memories of traditional food gathering.
Kʷukʷstéyp to Mandy Na'zinek Jimmie for her lifelong work with our elders
and community as a champion of our Nłeʔkepmxcin, our language. —NIC

In loving memory of Nc'icn
Aubrey Arnold Lezard —JF

NICOLA I. CAMPBELL

Words

A Day with Yayah

JULIE FLETT

Pictures

TRADEWIND BOOKS

VANCOUVER · LONDON

Yayah and Nikki were busy tanning deer hides just as a rainbow glimmered across the sky. Jamesie Pookins and Lenny came to visit from next door.

"My scmém'i?t," Yayah asked, "tell me which plants are ready in the springtime."

"Hékʷu? is wild rhubarb and c'ewéte?, wild celery," said Jamesie Pookins.

"And they are pronounced ha-kwoo and tse-weh-tah," added Nikki.

"Don't forget wild potatoes and lightning mushrooms," said Lenny. "Yayah, what are they called in our language?"

"Lightning mushrooms are called nki?kix̣qín and wild potatoes are called tetúwn'," Yayah answered. "Yes, you're right. Pronunciation is very important."

"Tah-too-wn and n-kee-keh-x-qiyn." They each practiced saying the X sound as though clearing their throats.

"Can we come gathering with you, Yayah?" asked Nikki.

"My scmém'i?t, you each have said you don't like to eat mushrooms."

"But we love gathering with you, Yayah!" Lenny and Jamesie exclaimed.

"S-cha-mem-eet means children," Nikki said, carefully pronouncing each syllable.

Every day the children learned new words, and scmém'i?t was yesterday's word.

Yayah quickly phoned their parents and packed lunch for everyone.

Nikki's braids were poofed out everywhere. "Oh my goodness, Nikki, your hair is a mess," said Yayah, re-braiding her hair. Then she put a scarf on Nikki's head.

Yayah wore a scarf too. Her braids were long and silver.

c'ewéte? • tetúwn' • scmém'i?t

Honk! Honk!

"Let's go!"

Everyone climbed into Auntie Karen's red minivan—Jamesie, Lenny, Nikki, Yayah, Grand-auntie Susan and Grand-uncle Chester.

"We always take the whole reserve everywhere we go," Nikki said.

"This isn't the whole reserve, my Nickel." Uncle Chester laughed. "We could easily fit four more."

The van drove past a pond, turned down a bumpy dirt road, and stopped. The scmém'i?t were excited.

"Keep your hats on. Watch out for wood ticks. And don't wander away."

"Okay, Yayah!" they sang out happily.

"Let's check if the hékʷu? and tetúwn' are ready first," said Yayah as she walked toward the pond.

The scmém'i?t followed, watching carefully for the tiny white flowers and the green shoots of hékʷu? growing along the edges of the pond. These tender new plants can only be harvested in the springtime.

hékʷu? • tetúwn'

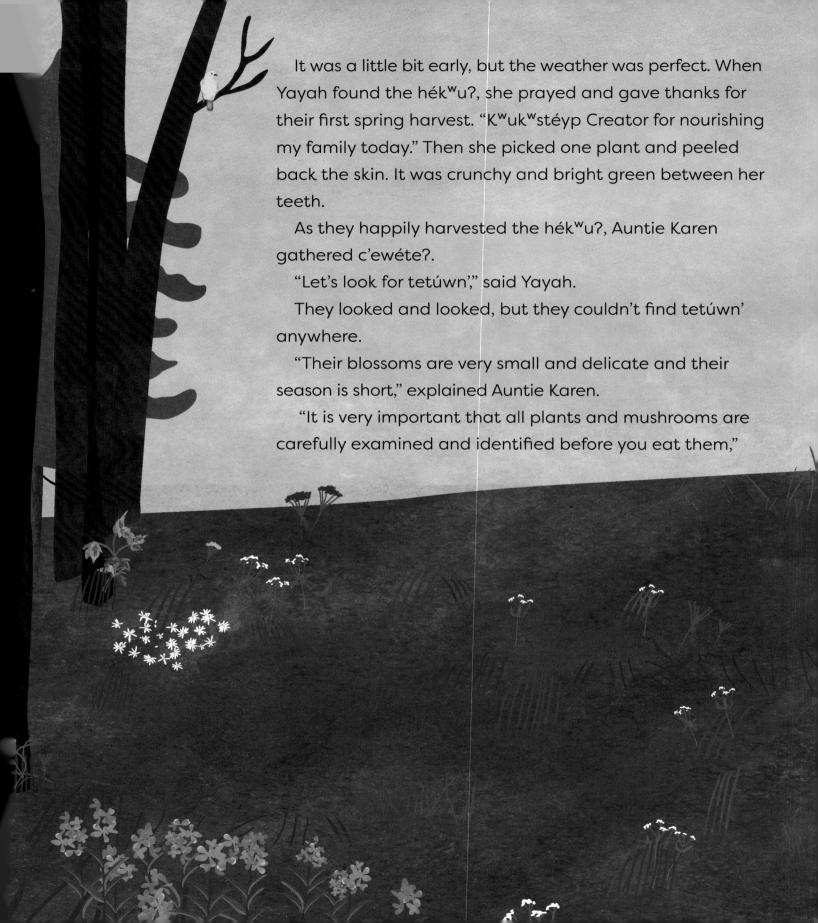

It was a little bit early, but the weather was perfect. When Yayah found the hékʷuʔ, she prayed and gave thanks for their first spring harvest. "Kʷukʷstéyp Creator for nourishing my family today." Then she picked one plant and peeled back the skin. It was crunchy and bright green between her teeth.

As they happily harvested the hékʷuʔ, Auntie Karen gathered c'ewéteʔ.

"Let's look for tetúwn'," said Yayah.

They looked and looked, but they couldn't find tetúwn' anywhere.

"Their blossoms are very small and delicate and their season is short," explained Auntie Karen.

"It is very important that all plants and mushrooms are carefully examined and identified before you eat them,"

Yayah explained. "Some plants are very poisonous. Does anyone see a poisonous plant nearby?"

The scmém'i?t looked everywhere. They saw fragrant pine trees, wildflowers, and tall grass. All around them the birds were singing. Then they saw some low shrubs with shiny, dark-green pointy-tipped leaves.

"Poison ivy!" all three kids hollered at once.

"Yes, don't touch the poison ivy," said Yayah. "It can cause a painful rash."

"You can treat the rash with cucumbers, oatmeal, or calamine lotion," said Nikki. "Right, Yayah?"

"Yes, my girl," Yayah answered. "But it depends on how severe the reaction is. Every person and every plant is different."

"Who knows what lightning mushrooms look like?" Yayah asked.

"They are golden brown—like marshmallows roasted on a willow stick." Jamesie was smiling.

"Right before it catches fire!" Lenny hollered.

Everyone laughed.

"Good remembering," said Auntie Karen. "Why are they called lightning mushrooms?"

"Because they grow on the grassy circles after lightning hits," Nikki answered.

"I see some," Lenny hollered.

nkiʔkix̣qín

The kids raced to the spot. Each of the scmém'i?t took a pinch of tobacco for an offering. Kneeling down, they said, "Kʷukʷstéyp Creator for feeding our loved ones today."

Then Jamesie sliced the base of the mushroom and held it up for everyone to see.

kʷukʷstéyp

"Who can tell me the name of this plant?" said Yayah, pointing to a patch of bright yellow flowers on the hillside.

"That's a sunflower," responded Lenny. "Sóx̣ʷm.'"

"They are also called arrowleaf balsamroot," said Nikki as she looked at the leaves and stem.

"We peel and eat the stems raw in the springtime," said Jamesie. "Or they can be steamed."

"That's right," said Yayah. "It looks similar to a wildflower called arnica. Arnica is a powerful medicine and isn't safe to eat."

"That's why it's important to correctly identify plants before you harvest them," said Nikki. "Right Yayah?"

"That's right."

sóx̣ʷm'

Pointing at a bush by the creek, Yayah asked, "What kind of bush is that?"

The kids looked closely at the leaves, and Lenny picked a dried-up furry berry.

"Silver willow," they answered.

"What is it good for?" asked Yayah.

"You soak them, scrub off the meat, and then, using a needle and thread, make the seeds into beads," Nikki said proudly. "Then we make necklaces out of them."

"What a beautiful day. In our language, qʷámqʷəmt means beautiful. Today we will learn the word qʷámqʷəmt," said Yayah.

"Qwam-qwem-t." The children carefully sounded out their new word.

"The qʷ sound is made at the back of your throat."

"Qʷámqʷəmt. It's a beautiful day!" said Nikki.

qʷámqʷəmt

"I'm hungry," said Lenny and Jamesie Pookins.
"Me too," agreed Yayah. When she found a good
log to picnic on, she hollered, "Ła?x̣ans! Lunchtime."
"Lh-aaah-hun-sh!" Nikki hollered.

Ła?x̣ans

After everyone sat down, Yayah handed out cups of hot sweet tea. Nikki gave everyone salmon sandwiches. "We looked everywhere for tetúwn', but we never found any," Karen said, disappointed.

"That's okay, my girl. They can be finicky," Yayah responded. "Now, what will we do with the riches from our tmíxʷ, our beautiful land?"

"I will jar my c'ewéte? and eat my hékʷu?," Auntie Karen said happily.

"We'll fry them up in butter as soon as we get home," Uncle Chester added.

"We need to save some for winter!" Auntie Susan scolded. "*We'll* be drying our mushrooms."

"Remember to check for wood ticks!" Jamesie Pookins shouted.

tmíxʷ

"I wish lightning mushrooms tasted like roasted marshmallows," said Nikki.

"Me too," Lenny agreed, holding up the biggest golden mushroom of all.

nki?kix̣qín

The sun shone bright and shadows danced through the red willows and cottonwood trees. An owl flew low overhead. The breeze was cool, with the warmth of spring. The scmém'i?t happily gifted their elders with the food they had gathered.

kʷukʷstéyp

Nɬeʔképmx

The Nɬeʔképmx Indigenous people are part of the Interior Salishan peoples and speak Nɬeʔkepmxcín. The Nɬeʔképmx of the Nicola Valley are often referred to as Scw'éxmx: People of the Creeks. They were historically referred to as Nlaka'pamux or Thompson River Salish. Their traditional territory encompasses the British Columbia Southern Interior (including the Fraser Canyon, Lytton, Spences Bridge, the Nicola Valley) and branches down to include parts of the North Cascades region of Washington. As a result of colonization and Indian residential school policies, many of our Indigenous languages in British Columbia and Canada are now considered critically endangered. Such is the case with Nɬeʔkepmxcín.

I am grateful for the opportunity to share my language with you.

kʷukʷscémxʷ

Nɬeʔkepmxcín Glossary of Words

Yéye
   Grandmother / Yayah *is an anglicized spelling.*

hékʷuʔ *(ha-kwoo)*
   wild rhubarb, also called cow parsnip

c'ewéteʔ *(tse-weh-tah)*
   wild celery

tetúwn' *(tah-too-wn)*
   wild potatoes, also called western spring beauty root

scmém'iʔt *(s-cha-mem-eet)*
   children / plural

kʷukʷstéyp *(kw-ookw-sh-tay-p)*
   thank you / This version of thank you is one that is said with honor and respect, for example elders and respected leaders. In this instance it is used while giving thanks to Mother Earth.

kʷukʷscémxʷ *(kw-ookw-sh-jam-x)*
   thank you / This version of thank you is for everyone.

qʷámqʷəmt *(qwam-qwem-t) The qw sound is made at the back of your throat.*
   beautiful, wonderful

ɬaʔxans *(lh-aaah-hun-sh) lh – slurpy L sound*
   time to eat

tmíxʷ *(tm-ee-xw)*
   our land, the land

nkiʔkix̣qín *(n-kee-keh-x-qiyn)*
   lightning mushrooms / Translates as 'thunderhead mushroom,' also called field or meadow mushroom.

sóx̣ʷm' *(sh-uxw-em) x – clearing throat sound*
   Wild sunflowers—also called arrowleaf balsamroot

Published by Tradewind Books in Canada and the UK in 2017
Text copyright © 2017 Nicola I. Campbell • Illustrations copyright © 2017 Julie Flett

Book design by Elisa Gutiérrez

The text of this book is set in Filson Soft and in various styles of the Catalina typeface family

10   9   8   7   6   5   4   3   2   1

· ·

LIBRARY AND ARCHIVES CANADA CATALOGUING IN PUBLICATION

Campbell, Nicola I., author

A day with Yayah / by Nicola Campbell ; Julie Flett, illustrator ; Tiffany

Stone, editor.

ISBN 978-1-926890-09-8 (hardcover)

I. Flett, Julie, illustrator II. Stone, Tiffany, 1967-, editor III. Title

PS8605.A5475D39 2017   jC813'.6   C2017-901834-5

· ·

Printed and bound
in Canada on ancient
forest-friendly paper.

The publisher thanks Keyan Zhang for her help with this project.

The publisher thanks the Government of Canada,
the Canada Council for the Arts and Livres Canada Books for their financial support.
We also thank the Government of the Province of British Columbia for the financial support it
has given through the Book Publishing Tax Credit program and the British Columbia Arts Council.